Library of Congress Cataloging-in-Publication Data

Schubert, Ingrid, 1953-
[Abracadabra. English]
Abracadabra / Ingrid & Dieter Schubert. – 1st American ed.
p. cm.

Summary: The forest animals unite to foil a mischievous wizard who has been casting spells on them.
ISBN 1-886910-17-0 (alk. paper)
[1. Wizards–Fiction. 2. Animals–Fiction. 3. Magic–Fiction.]
I. Schubert, Dieter, 1947– ill. II. Title.
PZ7.S3834Ab 1997
[E] – dc20
96-26691

Abracadabra

Ingrid and Dieter Schubert

FRONT STREET ❦ LEMNISCAAT

ARDEN, NORTH CAROLINA

Macrobius the Magician lived in a castle
on top of Brush Mountain.

The animals who lived far below in Shady Forest would often see him rummaging through the trees gathering glasswort, bottling bogdew, and munching mushrooms as he searched for ingredients for his magic recipes. They ignored him. He was just an ordinary magician who couldn't bother anyone.

Until, one day, he did. In fact, he bothered the whole forest. Every time an animal came by, Macrobius jumped from behind a bush, waved his magic wand, and shouted, "ABRACADABRA!"

He cast a spell on each and every animal he met.

The animals didn't much like the spells.

"I keep tripping over my ears," sniveled Hare.

"I feel like a fool with these wings," croaked Frog.

"Just look at my ears," hooted Owl.

All the animals had good reason to complain, and they did.

Something had to be done about Macrobius–soon!

"Has anybody seen Fox?" growled Bear. "He's so clever, he'll know what to do. Let's go see if he's home."

Fox heard the animals coming and met them as they arrived.

"Ah, Fox! We need your help," cawed Raven. "Macrobius
the Magician has gone crazy. Look what he's done to us!"

"I know," yipped Fox. "Listen to this."

"Yesterday I saw a big, fat goose near the brook. As I crept closer, the goose got bigger and fatter. Then when I was right behind it, *wham!*–the goose was gone and there stood Macrobius. He waved his wand and shouted 'ABRACADABRA!' and look at me now." Fox waddled out of his den.

In shock, the animals sniveled, croaked, hooted, growled, and generally made a racket. If clever Fox fell under Macrobius' spell, what hope was there?

Just then a small voice piped up. "Can I say something, please?
I have an idea." Everyone turned in surprise to Hedgehog. "You?"
"Yes, me!" he prickled. "Just listen to my plan."
All the animals gathered round. They liked Hedgehog's plan . . .

The next morning Macrobius woke up from pleasant dreams
of his magic pranks.

"This is sure more fun than bottling bogdew," he chortled.
"Today I'm really going to show them what I can do!"

He looked around for his magic wand but couldn't find it anywhere.
"Hmm. Where could I have put it?"

As if in answer to his question, he heard a noise—right inside his room.

"What's that? Who's there?" shouted Macrobius. "Where are you?"

Was it behind the curtain? He pulled it aside, but no one was there.

How about under the bed? No, not there.

Macrobius was getting angry—and nervous.

"I kn-kn-know you're in here," he shouted. "I'll—"

But before he could finish, the door of his closet flew open
with a loud bang and out burst an enormous beast, shrieking
and screeching. It rushed straight at Macrobius.

"Help!" he cried. "Mama!"

"Aaaaah!" piped the beast, in a surprisingly high voice. "I'm going to turn you into a mushroom, and you know what that means!"

"Nooooo!" screamed Macrobius, who knew that all magicians loved to eat wild mushrooms while gathering things in Shady Forest. He jumped out the window and ran down the mountain looking for someone–anyone– to save him from the beast.

Macrobius hid behind a tree, shivering, until he saw Fox and Hedgehog passing by.

"Dear Fox! Old friend Hedgehog! Please help! A terrible beast is after me. It's going to turn me into a mushroom."

"Ah, we know what you mean," said Fox.

"That's not good," agreed Hedgehog. "Especially because everyone knows that magicians love to eat mushrooms."

"Can you help me?" pleaded Macrobius. "I promise I won't cast any more spells on you. I didn't mean any harm."

"Well, maybe we could help if you really mean it."

"Oh, I will . . . I mean I won't . . . I mean I do. Oh, please help me."

"Okay, stay right there and don't move until we come back or else you'll be a mushroom for sure."

Macrobius stood behind the tree for a long, long time until finally Fox and
Hedgehog returned with all the other animals.

"Well, that's that," Hedgehog piped. "Here's your magic wand back.
Be careful with it."

"I will, I will. And the first thing I'll do is remove the spells I cast on you . . ."

"Not so fast," Frog said. "These wings are really quite handy."

"I'm getting fond of my ears, too," said Hare.

"Isn't there anything I can do to repay you for your help?" pleaded Macrobius.

"Anything?" Fox said, wiggling his webbed feet. "Well, I can think of something . . ."